QWERTYUIOP

A play by

Michael Yates

Nettle Books

Published 2016 by Nettle Books, Yorkshire

nettlebooks@hotmail.com
©2016 Michael Yates
ISBN: 978-0-9933729-1-9

Classification: Drama

The original production of <u>QWERTYUIOP</u> by The Charter Players took place at Featherstone Community Theatre and Powerhouse One theatre in Wakefield

Cast and technicians

Susan (35, pretty, prim) ....Catherine Pidd
Frankie (35, sexy, aggressive) ......Helen Watson
Mrs Baslow (55, overbearing) ....Freda Jones
Liz (35, lively)..........................Anne Eckersley
Pat (55, busybody).................Audrey Haggerty
Sandra (depressive)..................Mary Maxwell
Jenny...Mollie Dixon
Sally/Caroline (early 20s)............Emilie Watson
Alec (35, smart, middle class).........Eric Arundell
Des (35, loud, working class)...Andrew Sheppard

Director: Larraine Harrison
Stage management and lighting: Kate Dickinson
Sound: Jan and Philip Arundell
Plus June Shackleton, Tom Dixon and Janet Lunn

Financially supported by Wakefield District Arts

QWERTYUIOP is a tragicomedy set in the age of Margaret Thatcher about unemployed women joining a Government-sponsored training course to become shorthand typists.

By the time I'd actually written it, the play was very much an historical drama akin to (say) *The Merry Wives of Windsor* or at least *Hindle Wakes*. And typewriters were already artefacts of a bygone age.

So it's worth remembering that in those far-off times it really did happen that women with university degrees took courses in shorthand and typing as the first step on a ladder to executive positions which were otherwise denied them.

From such injustice and tyranny, the best jokes are often made. Because they cut deepest.

Michael Yates 2016

Furniture and props:

Furniture: 7 small wooden desks, 7 basic wooden chairs, one larger desk and larger more comfortable office chair, one coatstand, 1 small table, 2 armchairs, **Props:** various throws to change look of table and armchairs, 7 typewriters, 8 textbooks, 8 spiral bound notebooks, lots of A4 typing paper, two *NO SMOKING* signs, 1 teddy bear, 7 shopping bags, 1 pair boxer shorts, various parcels, Christmas streamers and tinsel.

ACT ONE

Scene 1

MUSIC: *RESPECT* BY ARETHA FRANKLIN.
THEN A CROCODILE OF "GIRLS" (FRANKIE,
SUSAN, SALLY, PAT, JENNY, LIZ AND ANN)
LED BY MRS BASLOW ENTERS STAGE RIGHT
IN FRONT OF THE CURTAIN. MRS BASLOW IS
PURPOSEFUL, THE OTHERS ARE LOOKING
ROUND, SLIGHTLY BEWILDERED. MUSIC
DIES. MRS BASLOW STOPS ABRUPTLY AT
STAGE CENTRE, TURNS AND ADDRESSES
THEM.

MRS BASLOW: I *know* you'll like it here. (SHE
GLANCES ROUND THE AUDITORIUM) It's such
a new, clean building. The council built it because
they wanted to bring industry here and they needed
more office space. So the rest of it won't be empty for
long, I'm sure.

(ENTER FROM STAGE LEFT SANDRA AT A
RUN, DROPPING HER BAGS, PICKING THEM
UP, GETTING AWKWARDLY INTO LINE AS
THE OTHERS LOOK ON BEMUSED)

MRS BASLOW (IGNORING HER): The council let
us rent the top floor because they were going to knock
down our old building to build a sports complex.
Sportarama, they called it. Then
they couldn't get the money for some reason, probably
to do with the government. Well, the government's
had a lot on its plate this year, sending all those

soldiers off to the Falklands. So now our *old* building is a peace centre. You can go there if you're unemployed and think peace is a good idea and want a cup of coffee or the use of a duplicator. It's amazing how people turn to duplicating when they're out of work. (SHE POINTS OUT ABOVE THE HEADS OF THE AUDIENCE AND THE GIRLS FOLLOW HER GAZE) We're on the ninth floor of course, and you can see the town hall from this window. (SHE POINTS) There. Where that red bus is. No, you've missed it. It's turned the corner. (SHE CONTINUES ACROSS THE STAGE, TALKING BACK OVER HER SHOULDER TO THE GIRLS WHO ARE FOLLOWING) And there's a wonderful view from the roof. It's so high and it's flat, you see. You can see right into the car park. (ALL EXIT STAGE LEFT).

Scene 2

THE CURTAIN RISES AS MRS BASLOW AND THE GIRLS ENTER STAGE LEFT INTO THE CLASSROOM. THERE ARE SEVEN DESKS WITH CHAIRS ARRANGED STAGE RIGHT IN TWO ROWS AND A TYPEWRITER ON EACH DESK. CENTRE STAGE BACK IS MRS BASLOW'S LARGER DESK WITH MORE COMFORTABLE CHAIR. THERE IS A COATSTAND STAGE LEFT. PRINTED *NO SMOKING* SIGNS ADORN A NUMBER OF THE DESKS.

MRS BASLOW: Welcome, girls, to the Castlefield School of Commerce. Every desk has its own typewriter and *some* of them have text books in the drawers. That means some of you without text books will have to share.   It might be advisable if you bought your own from the school shop. It would ease the pressure on the others. We advise it but we don't *insist* on it.

THE GIRLS MOOCH AROUND, HANG THEIR HATS AND COATS ON THE COAT STAND AND TENTATIVELY ARRANGE THEMSELVES IN THE DESKS AS FOLLOWS - BACK ROW LEFT TO RIGHT, JENNY, PAT, SALLY, SANDRA; FRONT ROW LEFT TO RIGHT, LIZ, FRANKIE, ANN, SUSAN.

JENNY (LOOKING ROUND THE DESKS): There are no *electric* typewriters.

MRS BASLOW: Some of you may have noticed there are no *electric* typewriters. There's a reason for that. It's because we want you to get used to all kinds of typewriters, not just the latest models. Some of you, when you get jobs, will be joining small firms who can't afford expensive electrical equipment. You wouldn't want to take your driving test in a car with automatic gears now, would you?

JENNY: But we will get the *chance* to use electric?

MRS BASLOW: Oh yes. Later on. Yes. (DROPS HER VOICE) I'm *sure* you will. Now (TO CLASS AS A WHOLE) I'm Mrs Baslow and I'm your teacher for typing and shorthand. I'm sure we're going to get along like a house on fire. Like a block of flats on fire, in fact. Here at the school we pride ourselves on our good relations with our students. Most of them are *private* students, of course, who pay their own

7

fees. But times are hard, as I'm sure we all know. That's why we decided to offer our skills to this wonderful government scheme to re-train unemployed people. *Unwaged,* I suppose I should say. And you are our pioneers, our very first class, so all eyes are on you. It's going to be hard work because the course you'll be doing normally takes a year and we have to get it all into three months. (GASPS OF DISMAY FROM THE GIRLS) So I intend to have regular tests every week to keep you up to scratch. And once in a while I just may throw in a *very extra special* test without warning, so look out! (PAUSE) You know, it's only a matter of being willing to make the effort. Oh, one little thing... (TO FRANKIE) You, dear, what's your name?

FRANKIE (SURPRISED, SMILING): Mrs Maddock. Frankie.

MRS BASLOW: Ah. Frankie. That will be short for Frances. Though, of course, it's not really short at all. Now, Frances, I hope you won't mind my saying this, but when you're working in an office... well, it's not the same as working in a factory, is it? We have to watch our appearance, and we might as well get it right, start as we mean to go on. You must understand there's no school rule against trousers *as such*, but lots of employers don't like to see their young ladies dress that way. I take it you do *own* a skirt?

FRANKIE: Yes. Well, last time I looked in the wardrobe...

MRS BASLOW: Excellent. Anyway, skirts are so much more becoming to the fuller figure, don't you think? Now, sit down, all of you and we'll get to know each other.

FRANKIE (IN WHISPER, TO LIZ ON HER LEFT) : Actually, these are our Des's jeans. I prefer a *man's* jeans. They feel stronger. In Des's case, they *smell* stronger too.

MRS BASLOW (RAISING HER VOICE): This is the moment when I always feel a bit like Julie Andrews in that film. Now, you on the left - tell me your name, dear.

JENNY: Mrs Harvey. (PAUSE) Jenny.

MRS BASLOW: *Jenny.* And you, dear?

PAT: Mrs Richards. Pat.

MRS BASLOW: *Pat.* And...

SALLY: Sally Busby.

MRS BASLOW: *Sally.*

SANDRA (WITHOUT EXPRESSION): Sandra.

MRS BASLOW: *Sandra.*

LIZ: Elizabeth. (PAUSE) Liz.

MRS BASLOW: *Elizabeth.* Now (TO FRANKIE) you did tell me yours, dear, and it's...

FRANKIE: Frankie.

MRS BASLOW: Of course. And... (INDICATES NEXT)

ANN: Ann, Mrs Baslow.

SUSAN: Susan, Mrs Baslow.

MRS BASLOW: There. That wasn't painful, was it? I'm sure I'll remember them all later. (PAUSE) Now - typing. The first thing I want you to do is take a good look at your typewriter. Go on. There it is. Take a really good look. Right. Now look away. *Quickly!* (CLAPS HANDS) Now - I never want to see you look at your typewriter ever again. No. I mean that. Instead, I want you to open your text books at page five, which is the diagram of the typewriter keyboard. There's a little exercise on the opposite page that I want you to try. Just a few sentences specially designed to stretch your fingers. Type, type, type. Without looking at the typewriter. Look at the diagram and just *feel* your way. (WAVES HER HANDS AS THOUGH USING A KEYBOARD) Feel, feel, feel... No peeping now!

ANN: Please, Mrs Baslow, can we look to put the paper in?

MRS BASLOW: Of course, dear. As long as you don't look at the *keys*. I suppose I'll just have to *trust* you. (SHE GOES TO HER DESK AT THE BACK OF THE CLASSROOM).

IN THE FOLLOWING SEQUENCE AND IN SIMILAR SEQUENCES THROUGHOUT THE

PLAY, THE GIRLS MAKE SILENT TYPING
MOTIONS WITH THEIR FINGERS WHILE THEY
FACE THE AUDIENCE AND RECITE THEIR
EXERCISES IN SING-SONG VOICES, EACH IN
TURN).

JENNY: Diana said killing in pain was a sin...

PAT: Ian fails in singing, Gillian in hiking...

SALLY: Jack fled for his life on dirty dark roads...

ANN: Idleness is foolish, learn a good skill...

LIZ: Dirty dense fog falls on hills and dales alive.
(REALISES HER MISTAKE) *Alike.*

MRS BASLOW: Every correction to be done *three*
times.

LIZ (FURIOUSLY, WITH FINGER ACTION TO
MATCH) *Alike, alike, alike...!*

FRANKIE: The crazy paving was quickly fixed by
the jolly gardener...

ANN: On the shores of Lake Kyanga live Kenya's
smallest tribe...

SUSAN: Diana has a keen head and lean hands...

JENNY: Jack Flash lags while nifty Nan sells jade...

PAT: Jan keeps ten hens; she sells eggs, carrots and
kale...

SALLY: Gails lash lakes, hail slashes sledges. Oh!
Hedges, hedges, hedges...!

ANN: For love of the dove, David died...

LIZ: A sad lad has a hard head and a bad back...

FRANKIE: Gale sells jade and eel. *And ale, and ale, and ale!*

ANN: A bad dad sells ale in the sale...

SUSAN: A sad lad and his dad had a bad fall...

JENNY: A bad lass had a sad fall. All lads have dads...

PAT: A lass had a sash. Dad had Alaska salad...

SALLY: All ash falls in a flash on David...

ANN: Not all lads' fads have made dads glad...

LIZ: A sad lass shall dash as all hail falls...

FRANKIE: A bad lad shall pass as all halls fail...
SHE SIGHS, COLLECTS HER HANDBAG AND
COAT AND MAKES FOR THE FRONT OF THE
STAGE

ANN: Hail lashed the Lakeland pass...

SUSAN: The bad lad fished as the sad dad pissed. (REALISES MISTAKE, THEN, FURIOUS AND EMBARRASSED) *Passed, passed, passed!*

FRANKIE (PASSING SUSAN'S DESK) I can see we'll be having our problems with you, my girl. She'll be washing your mouth out with correction fluid.

SHE FLICKS SUSAN'S HAIR RIBBON, THEN CONTINUES WALKING TO FRONT OF STAGE AS CURTAINS CLOSE BEHIND HER. SHE ADDRESSES THE AUDIENCE

FRANKIE: Well, that was an eye-opener and no mistake. I was really sorry I had to leave early to see the dentist about my molars. Mr Little, he's called, but I always think of him as Mr Spittle. Actually, they're not really bad as teeth go, but I like to get high on a spot of novacaine now and again. Otherwise, I'd've stayed late. Just to sneak a look at my typewriter keys after hours. Or say something scathing to the one with the hair ribbon, the one that blushes a lot. I bet when she buys Tampax, she wears dark glasses. (PAUSE) There. I can see you've got me pegged by now. Troublemaker. School bully. God, I'm dying for a smoke. I've just got time for a quick one before Mr Spittle starts poking about in my mouth. He'll tell me to give it up. *That* and sweets. He always does. (EXIT STAGE LEFT)

Scene 3

MUSIC: *EVERY LITTLE THING SHE DOES IS MAGIC* BY THE POLICE. THEN CURTAIN UP ON FRANKIE'S FRONT ROOM. DES IS FRONT

STAGE RIGHT, IN THE ONE OF TWO
ARMCHAIRS, STUDYING HIS POOLS COUPON.
THERE IS A SMALL TABLE AT BACK STAGE
CENTRE. MUSIC DIES. ENTER FRANKIE
STAGE LEFT. SHE IS DRESSED AS BEFORE -
JEANS AND SHIRT - BUT NO COAT AND NOW
SHE HAS BARE FEET. SHE IS CARRYING A
TEDDY BEAR.

FRANKIE (SHOUTING OFFSTAGE LEFT): Don't
let me catch you doing that again or I'll tell your
father! (THEN IN QUIETER VOICE) Goodnight.
Godbless.

SHE THROWS TEDDY ONTO TABLE, SITS
DOWN AT TABLE WHICH IS STREWN WITH
PAPERS, AND LIGHTS CIGARETTE. AFTER A
PAUSE SHE TURNS TO DES

FRANKIE: Darren's been peeing on the bathroom
floor again.

DES (NOT BOTHERING TO LOOK UP): I'll give
him a clout tomorrow.

FRANKIE (PICKS UP HOMEWORK BOOK,
LIGHTS CIGARETTE): It's three days now. You
haven't asked me how it's going, Des.

DES (STILL NOT LOOKING UP) You what?

FRANKIE: My typing course. How it's going.

DES (STILL NOT LOOKING UP): Oh yeah. How is
it then?

FRANKIE: Well, thanks for asking. It's OK really.

DES: That's nice. (LOOKS UP AT LAST) Well, I don't suppose there's much to it really. *I've* been in offices enough times to see what goes on. I mean, every time I drive the truck somewhere new, I do the unloading, then I go up to the office, wherever it is, and get the chit signed. And whatever sort of office it turns out to be, there's always some young lass with red fingernails making tea. I know what typists are. Though I don't know what good it'll do you in the end.

FRANKIE: You don't think I'll get a job then? Well, I don't suppose I *will*. It's a bit of extra money for now though, isn't it? They're giving me £50 a week, the government are. That's about the same as I'd actually earn if I got a job afterwards. Still, I'll try not to let it change my life.

DES (TAKING THE BAIT): Oh, come on! I don't know what you need more money for! It's not as if *I* don't earn good money. There's blokes would give their right arms to be a driver like me, going all around the country earning my sort of money.

FRANKIE: Oh, I know they all look up to you, them other drivers. They always have a good word for Rubber Duck (SHE PUTS ON HER GLASSES)

DES: Anyway, you've already got a job.

FRANKIE (TAKES OFF HER GLASSES AGAIN):
Looking after Viscount Linley upstairs? Don't I know
it!

DES: There's nowt wrong with looking after kids. My
mother always did OK.

FRANKIE: Yeah. Never a day off in 30 years. And
look what she got to show for it.

DES: Gerrawaywithyer. (LOOKS BACK AT
COUPON) We've not won owt. I didn't think we had,
but I've only just found t'coupon.

FRANKIE: That's a blow. What else is new?
(SUDDEN SCREAMS AND SHOUTS ARE
HEARD FROM UPSTAIRS) That's not new either.

DES (AFTER A PAUSE OF ABOUT 90 SECONDS
WHILE THE SCREAMS CONTINUE): It's Darren.

FRANKIE: I *know* it's Darren. I know who it *is*. I
know it's not cats fighting. But I'm trying to do my
homework. It's my shorthand homework and I'm
trying to do it for tomorrow. (SCREAMS STOP)
Wait. I think he's stopped. (SCREAMS START UP
AGAIN) I could stuff his mouth with dirty
underpants. There's enough of them lying around up
there. That's another thing - I've got to do some
washing tonight.

DES: Oh, you are *hard* sometimes, Frankie. Real hard
for a woman. He's screaming his head off.

FRANKIE: I don't see *you* jumping up.

DES: I've been at work all day, haven't I?

FRANKIE: OK. No help for it then. Muggins is elected again. (PUTS OUT CIGARETTE, PICKS UP TEDDY BEAR) I'll see if John Selwyn Gummer here can do any good. (

FRANKIE EXITS STAGE LEFT. DES PUTS DOWN HIS COUPON, CHECKS HIS WATCH, AND, FACING THE AUDIENCE, SWITCHES ON AN INVISIBLE TV SET. WE HEAR THE OPENING THEME OF *THE SWEENEY*.

DES (PICKING UP COUPON ONE LAST TIME AND SCREWING IT UP): Bloody Leeds United! Still, if they did any better, they'd have to turn professional. (HE SETTLES DOWN TO WATCH TV. THE SCREAMING UPSTAIRS SUDDENLY STOPS)

FRANKIE (RE-ENTERING WITHOUT TEDDY): Quiet at last. He only wanted to tell me the plaster had come off his toe. He was licking it to stick it back on again. (SHE RESUMES HER SEAT AT TABLE, FIDDLES ABOUT WITH PEN AND PAPER, THEN:) Look, Des, is it going to be like this all night? I've got work to do. I'm not just sitting down to rest my varicose veins.

DES (ENGROSSED IN TV): So what am *I* supposed to do?

FRANKIE (LEAPING UP AND RUNNING ACROSS): What can you *do?* I suppose there's not much left. *I* cooked the tea. *I* washed up. *I* put Darren to bed. Oh yes, one little thing. You could turn off this rubbish. (SHE TURNS THE TV OFF) *I* can tell you what'll happen. There'll be a hard looking bloke in a leather jacket - Inspector Reagan and the other one will chase him across a building site and knock the shit out of him.

DES (STARTLED, LOOKING ROUND): Have you seen it before?

FRANKIE: It's always the same. They always chase somebody across a building site and knock the shit out of him. I think the director's got shares in Wimpey.

DES: Aw, you *do* talk rubbish. Anyway, I've just thought - I helped lay the table for tea.

FRANKIE: You put the pickles out. You're the only one that *eats* pickles.

DES (LEAPS ANGRILY TO HIS FEET): Right, missus - I can see you're spoiling for a row. Now, I don't ask much when I come home from a hard day's graft, all I ask is a sit-down in front of the telly for an hour before I go to bed. I don't think that's too much to ask. I don't hear any complaints when it comes to handing over me money every week. Oh no, it's a different story then.

FRANKIE: I've never criticised your earning power, Des. There's two things about you I never dare criticise and one of them's your earning power. And I know we've got to be grateful in these hard times that you've got a job at all...

DES (FURIOUS): *Got a job at all!* Listen, sunshine, this one here'll never be out of work no matter how long that Tory bitch stays in power! I'm senior driver, top man. People will always need transport and they'll always need a good man to drive. It's not me who's going to be replaced by a bloody word compressor! Typists! Bloody useless lot! I know. I've been in offices. I've seen them. Dirty as well, if you ask me. I've seen enough of typists with their pictures of pop stars on the walls, stripped to the waist and playing with their microphones. And the older ones are the worst - the ones with the corsets and the pearls. Then it's Charles Bronson with his shirt off and a feather in his cowboy hat! If I was the boss, I wouldn't let them put up things like that!

FRANKIE (IN EXAGGERATED TONE): What a disturbing picture you paint of the world of commerce! What about the tart with the boobs you've got hanging in the cab? The one wearing fishnet stockings and nothing else and carrying a hosepipe? I suppose that's not dirty, that's good clean fun.

DES (DEFENSIVELY): Well, it's useful, that picture is. It's a calendar. And it's not a hosepipe she's holding, it's a folding umbrella. It's April when the showers come and the umbrella's sort of symbolic. That just shows how your mind works!

FRANKIE: If it's calendars you want, there's one with views of Switzerland in the kitchen that I'll give you

for nowt! Aw, Des... (THE TONE OF HER VOICE
CHANGES AND SHE COMES OVER AND HUGS
HIM) Let's not have rows, not on me shorthand
homework night. I know you work hard, love, and
you've a right to your boobs. I suppose it's not all fun
being a glamorous model. I bet she has to have her
stretch marks painted out. Listen... you know that
washing machine you bought me last Christmas out of
our savings? That smashing, fully automated, state-of-
the-art product of modern technology that the man
came and fixed again last week? Well, look. All I
need is some big strong man to go upstairs and walk
around picking up a few bits of dirty washing that
might be lying about here and there and then come
down and put the lot into that great big washing
machine. Just for Frankie, eh? And then, when you've
turned the dial to Q and got the whole thing going,
you can come back and watch them run across the
building site and knock shit out of anybody they
catch. And in the meantime I'll be getting on with my
homework and that'll mean I'll be coming to bed that
much sooner, won't I? (SHE RUBS HERSELF
AGAINST HIM) Then you can get that other big
machine of yours going.

DES (SUBDUED): OK. OK then. (HE WALKS
ACROSS STAGE LEFt) I don't mind doing my share,
you know. All you've got to do is ask. I mean... you
don't have to bring sex into it every time you're losing
the argument.

EXIT DES. FRANKIE RETURNS TO THE
TABLE, SITS DOWN AND STARTS WORK

20

FRANKIE (TO AUDIENCE AFTER ABOUT A MINUTE): I don't know why *you're* still here. It must be very boring watching somebody work. (PAUSE) You know, I *can't* work. Not now. (GETS UP, RUBS HER EYES, COMES TO FRONT OF CURTAIN AS IT CLOSES BEHIND HER) I've not got a scholarly attitude, that's what Miss Kendrick always used to say. She was my form teacher at Addlethorpe High. Or Addlethorpe Low as we used to call it. But I'm not really stupid, I'm just not *amenable*. That's what Miss Kendrick used to say: Frankie, you're not amenable to discipline. Or English. Or maths. Or history. Or anything much. Of course, I was always amenable to *some* things, from an early age. But I won't name them in mixed company. (PAUSE) Yeah. *Too* amenable, now I think about it. Otherwise, I'd be married to Clint Eastwood or Sylvester Stallone instead of our Des. Lying by the swimming pool in Beverly Hills with the outside air conditioner on, instead of stuck in the living room in Attlee Crescent doing daft squiggles in a notebook. Maybe she was right. Miss Kendrick, I mean. Maybe I should've been more amenable where it mattered. *Yes miss, no miss and please can I give out the milk?* (PAUSE) No. It doesn't sound like me, does it? Like I said, school bully, that's me. Troublemaker. Always was, always will be. You were right first time. Oh, I'll make that one with the hair ribbon wish she'd never seen a piece of carbon paper, see if I don't!

EXIT STAGE LEFT

Scene 4

MUSIC: *WELCOME TO THE HOUSE OF FUN* BY MADNESS. CURTAIN OPENS ON THE CLASSROOM. MUSIC DIES. THE GIRLS SIT AT THEIR DESKS, COPYING INTO SHORTHAND NOTEBOOKS AS MRS BASLOW, STAGE FRONT, DICTATES TO THEM IN THE OVER-EMPHATIC TONE AND ARTIFICIAL PAUSES RESERVED FOR THIS KIND OF OPERATION

MRS BASLOW: The invention of shorthand / brought with it/ wonderful opportunities/ for self advancement comma/ and the ability to write shorthand/ has been one of the stepping stones/ to success/ for many a famous man comma/ or woman full point (PAUSE AS FRANKIE ENTERS STEALTHILY STAGE LEFT, WEARING SKIRT, AND SETTLES IN HER SEAT) I will now continue. Its usefulness and value/ in all walks and areas of life/ is so self-evident/ as not to be questioned comma/ and a knowledge of the skill/ is an asset of great value/ to everyone comma/ whether young or old comma/ rich or poor...

FRANKIE (INTERRUPTING IN STAGE WHISPER) In sickness and in health...

MRS BASLOW (IGNORING HER): ... in private comma/ commercial comma/ or professional life full point... (PAUSE) Now. You. Susan, isn't it? How well did you do with that?

SUSAN: Not very well, Mrs Baslow. I got lost around *knowledge.*

MRS BASLOW (JOKILY): Well, knowledge is the very thing we're here to help you with. (TO THE CLASS AS A WHOLE): Hand your books in and I'll mark them. (PAT LEAPS UP AND COLLECTS THE BOOKS AND GIVES THEM TO MRS BASLOW) While I'm doing that, you can turn to your typing exercise. I know some of you find typing a little bit easier than shorthand. But don't worry. You'll be as right as ninepence in both before you know it.

MRS BASLOW GOES TO HER DESK AT THE BACK AND BEGINS TO MARK THE BOOKS. FROM THE AMOUNT OF MARKS SHE IS MAKING AND FROM THE LOOK ON HER FACE, WE SEE THE GIRLS HAVE NOT DONE WELL. IN THE FOREGROUND, THEY GO THROUGH THE TYPING SEQUENCE AS BEFORE

JENNY: Sarah sent her cousin Jim a long letter telling him about artichokes she had seen in Ireland...

PAT: It is good to see foreign goods on offer here while we sell firm favourites in far-off countries...

SANDRA: My friends Jane and Julian are planning to join the Spen Valley Badminton Club founded by James B. Hardcastle...

SUSAN: Any attempt to describe the pattern of life in the Isle of Man today must have regard to what is permanent in the environment and what is in the process of change...

LIZ: In the recent heatwave, we sold a record 73 pairs of sandals in three days...

FRANKIE: Our previous best was 36 pairs in seven days. That was three years ago...

ANN: Maureen says seven people will be coming on the picnic on August the third...

SUSAN: We shall meet at my mouse - *house, house, house* - at 73 Park Lane, and drive 37 miles in three mini cars...

JENNY: On July the seventh, our local cricket team beat its nearest rival by 373 runs to 337...

PAT: When our captain went into bat, there were three wickets down for 37 and he saved the day with a fine innings of 73...

SALLY: After that, our team scored steamily. *Steadily, steadily, steadily.* The last man added a another 37...

SANDRA: Out of our seven second cousins, four celebrated their eighth birthday on May the fourth...

LIZ: Bill has 48 flats to rent and eight to sell. Only four have garages...

FRANKIE: Mother likes sewing and has made herself shirts and hats as well as briefs and brass. *Briefs and bras, briefs and bras, briefs and bras!*

ANN: The eight late crates contained four broken vases and 48 chipped plates...

SUSAN: In order number 448 we asked for four pairs of gloves and eight shits. Aaaghhh!! *Shirts, shirts, shirts!* (CLASS COLLAPSES WITH LAUGHTER)

MRS BASLOW (ANGRILY): Susan, you should be more careful... Remember - if we wish to do things quickly, we must always take our time.

SUSAN (EXTREMELY EMBARRASSED): Sorry, Mrs Baslow. (FRANKIE MOUTHS THE "SORRY, MRS BASLOW" AND SUSAN GLARES AT HER ANGRILY)

MRS BASLOW: Very well. Continue.

JENNY: It takes a sound song to make a music-lover mellow…

PAT: The song is ended but the tune still cheers…

SANDRA: Singing and dancing are a natural combination…

SUSAN: But talking and walking are equally compatible…

LIZ: Walking in the wild is a way of wearing out one's shoes…

FRANKIE: Waking in the wet is wearisome when it rains…

ANN: Driving rain is made of drops not drips…

SALLY: The rhythm of the rain is a sad, sad song…

JENNY: Two wrongs do not make a right…

PAT: One swallow does not a summer make…

SANDRA: Two swallows will not a strong thirst slake…

SUSAN: Baking bread in summer is thirsty work…

LIZ: A loaf of bread, a jug of wine and thou…

FRANKIE: Give me a pigsfoot and a bottle of beer…

ANN: Temperance is the most timorous of virtues…

SALLY: Temporary can mean virtually permanent…

SUSAN: Any attempt to describe the pattern of life in the Isle of Man today must have regard to what is permanent in the environment and what is in the process of change...

FRANKIE: Sarah sent her cousin Jim a long, long letter telling him about artichokes she had seen in Ireland...

MRS BASLOW (TO THE GIRLS AS A WHOLE) Just carry on working till you've finished your task.

MRS BASLOW PICKS UP THE BOOKS AND WALKS FORWARD TO FRONT OF STAGE AS

THE GIRLS "FREEZE" INTO IMMOBILITY AND
SILENCE. MRS BASLOW ADDRESSES THE
AUDIENCE

MRS BASLOW: Teaching. (PAUSE) It's a wonderful
thing. But, you know, there's one thing more
wonderful than teaching. Who knows what it is?
(SHE LOOKS ROUND THE AUDIENCE) Come on,
who can tell me the one thing that's even more
wonderful than teaching? (PAUSE) Of course, I
know I can ask you that sort of question without
having to worry about the answer. I mean, if you ask
a lot of *young* people that sort of question these days,
you risk letting yourself in for a mouthful of smut. I
know about young people. I've raised three of my
own. And I'm a grandmother, though I know I don't
look it. That's why it's nice to teach older girls. Well,
let's say *mature students*. (PAUSE) Oh, I can see I'm
going to have to tell you. What it is that's even more
wonderful than teaching. Right. It's *learning*. Of
course, a lot of you will have known that. It was just
on the tip of your tongue. But speaking out in front of
other people is difficult, isn't it? So many people
don't have the confidence to do that. And really it's
the job of a good teacher to give you confidence. Here
- I'll give you a leaflet about the school and its work.
The fees are very reasonable. (PAUSE AS SHE
THROWS OUT THE LEAFLETS) But I love
teaching. I love to see other people blossoming
around me. Growing. Learning what a wonderful
thing it is to learn. And you never stop learning,
especially when you're a teacher. Look at this class
I'm teaching now. Being... more mature, they're
also... well, more set in their ways. Now, some slip of
a girl comes into class and she's just 17, and she's not

got much upstairs. But if the teacher has got the right furniture ready and waiting, well, you can just move it in straight away. These more mature ones, on the other hand, they've already got some furniture and it's not all very good. Most of it from MFI, if you know what I mean. Looks smart for a few months then the veneer starts to peel away. And sometimes it's difficult to get people to give up their old bits of what I call *mental plywood*. So that's a challenge for the teacher, isn't it? That's what I mean by learning. Learning to adapt to your pupils. Oh yes, I wouldn't change places, not even with Princess Diana. (LOOKS AT WATCH) Is that really the time? It's allright for these girls - they can have a nice little break now. All on the taxpayer too. But I've still got this marking to do.

SHE WAVES AND EXITS STAGE LEFT.

MUSIC: GIRLS ON FILM BY DURAN DURAN. AS THE MUSIC PLAYS, THE GIRLS START TO MOVE AGAIN, LIKE RIP VAN WINKLES COMING AWAKE. THEY STRETCH, YAWN ETC, THEN SIT OR STAND IN THE MIDDLE OF THE CLASS IN AN INFORMAL GROUP. THE MUSIC DIES.

PAT: I'll get them. I know these machines. (POINTS TO EACH OF THE WOMEN IN TURN) That's chocolate, chocolate, tea with, tea without, tea without either, chocolate and tea with both. Three sixes, two 27s and a 28.

SHE GOES OUT STAGE RIGHT WITH A TRAY

SALLY (to the remaining pupils): Have you *tasted* the tea?

LIZ: That's why I'm having the chocolate. (PAUSE) Allright, let's hear it (TO THEM ALL) What brought you lot to Colditz? What did you do to deserve it, eh? I'll tell you my confession. I'm a French teacher. No jokes about private lessons, OK? I actually had a job once. In a secondary modern, so you can tell how long ago that was. The only place they need French teachers these days is in Zaire and I know because I've been through the alphabet. But I don't think I could ever leave England - I'd miss the climate. (HUGS HERSELF AND SHIVERS)

FRANKIE (LIGHTING A CIGARETTE): Why are there never any ashtrays? Here, pass us the bin.

SALLY (PASSING HER THE BIN): It *is* parky in here, isn't it? I wonder why they don't put the heating on. It *is* November after all. I think I'll put my coat on.

SUSAN (TO FRANKIE): I think it's because you're not allowed to smoke. I mean, why there aren't any ashtrays. There are signs all around. (SHE GETS AN AGGRESSIVE STARE FROM FRANKIE, SO HURRIEDLY CHANGES THE SUBJECT) I agree about the heating. Perhaps we should complain...

FRANKIE: *You* complain then. Though I'd wait until I was in her good books again, if I were you. She thinks you've got a dirty mind, what with all that shitting and pissing you go on about.

ANN (TO LIZ): Being a teacher must be very interesting. All I was doing in my old job was filing. So I volunteered for redundancy to come here.

SALLY (TO ANN): Didn't your husband mind? Not having the money coming in?

ANN: It wasn't any more than this.

SALLY: But this won't last long.

ANN: Anyway, I'm not married. I only wear this (INDICATES RING) because of Robin. He's my little boy. He's 18 months. Our mom looks after him.

PAT (RETURNING WITH PLASTIC CUPS WHICH THEY TAKE EAGERLY): There's oxtail soup. I didn't know there was oxtail soup. It's a very good machine. Now then, what have I missed? I can see we're all having a lovely chat.

FRANKIE: Just discussing life's rich tapestry, the meaning of it all. With me, it's definitely force of circumstance, why I'm here. I need the money for little personal things like paying the rent. Though I wouldn't tell our Des we had money problems. He's never learned to count in double figures.

PAT (SHOCKED): Force of circumstance? Well, nobody's forced *me* to come here, I can assure you. I jumped at the chance. Not that I don't enjoy being at home with Anthea and Dominic. They're our children. But they're older now and I think it does youngsters good to do things for themselves. I just think every woman should have an outside interest, something to keep her fresh. You know. It's a way of keeping the magic alive. So the husband benefits as well. And the husband should have an outside interest too. If the husband has an outside interest, it keeps the magic alive for his wife. My Arthur's a very keen gardener.

LIZ: You can't get more outside than that.

FRANKIE: I'd always know if our Des had an outside interest. He'd start wearing clean underpants.

PAT: There's no need to be vulgar.

SUSAN (EAGERLY): But *work* is a man's outside interest, isn't it? That's why men take themselves so seriously. And it should be the same for women. I mean, women have a right to have interesting jobs like men. I used to work in a library...

JENNY (INTERRUPTING): I don't see that stamping books is very interesting. My Brett works in a hospital. He's a porter. That's not very interesting either.

FRANKIE: Doesn't he get to save lives once in a while, dashing up in the nick of time with an oxygen cylinder?

JENNY: I don't think so. I've never heard him mention it. All he talks about is emptying pigswill and dirty dressings and how they bring in the road crash cases with their eyes hanging out...

FRANKIE: I *like* a man who makes you laugh.

SUSAN (TO JENNY): But that *is* interesting, isn't it? In a way. I mean… It's real. It's life and death. It makes you realise what life is all about.

JENNY: He says it puts him off his dinner.

PAT: Well, it would, wouldn't it? I mean, people's eyes hanging out. I don't think *that's* what life's about. Not people's eyes hanging out.

LIZ: It's not about the jolly gardener fixing the crazy paving. Or Jane and Julian joining the badminton club. It's not like the stuff we're typing day in day out.

PAT: Well, I don't agree. After all, we're just beginners. And even when you think about the sentences we've done already - well, you must learn *something* from them. If you've got an open mind. And it gets more interesting as you go on. I've been reading ahead. There's passages about business and commerce and the weather and how poetry is good for you. I know we're not sort of learning them for what's in them, but it's all very interesting if you're fresh. I think it's very good.

SANDRA (ALWAYS TALKS IN A MONOTONE): I think it's boring. I think this place is boring. I think life is boring. That's what *I* think. I've tried to kill myself twice.

PAT (AFTER A BRIEF EMBARRASSED SILENCE): Well, I'm sure it was only a cry for help, wasn't it, dear?

SUSAN (CHANGING THE SUBJECT): I think Pat's right in a way. It's bound to get more interesting as we go along. After all, learning shorthand is like learning another language, isn't it? And typing... well, it's very useful even if you *can't* get a job. I can start typing Alec's notes for work...

PAT: Oh, what does he do?

SUSAN: He's a lecturer... (CATCHES HERSELF) a *teacher* at the polytechnic. English and drama.

FRANKIE: Very nice. And no children to mither you, I'll be bound. Easy to see *you* don't need the money.

SUSAN: He's not that well paid. Anyway, I'm determined to get a job. Women need their independence.

FRANKIE: *I* don't. *I* don't need independence. I want to be kept. Preferably at the level to which Joan Collins has become accustomed.

SUSAN: But being independent is what gives a woman equality.

FRANKIE: I had you pegged as a women's libber even before I knew what your husband did for a living. I don't want equality, ta very much. Do you think I'd want to be equal with our Des, with a lorry driver that brings home £100 a week basic - a hundred and twenty if he works all the hours God sends? Give it a rest. I'm superior to our Des. He'd be lost without me to tell him where to find a clean pair of socks or even when to put some on. He'd go to work and stink.

If I ever left him, all he'd eat would be toast because that's all he knows how to make. If you asked him to boil an egg, he'd expect a recipe. No, I don't want to be equal with Des. And I don't want our Darren to be like Des when *he* grows up. I'm bringing him up like a girl to have a bit of sense.

SALLY: Is there *any* man you'd like to be equal with?

FRANKIE: I wouldn't mind being equal with Robert Redford for a couple of hours. Though I might let him get on top of me now and again. But really, I don't give a shit for men, borrowing a word from madam over there (INDICATING SUSAN). I mean, I *like* them - don't get the wrong idea. I've never been one of them that want to start up communes with all girls together and talk about dustbinpersons. No. I like men, I really do. I like our Des the way I like spaghetti hoops. They're easy to warm up and I'm used to the flavour. But honestly, women make too much fuss over men. It's our disadvantage, the way we keep going on about them.

SUSAN: *You're* the one that's doing all the talking. I always suspect there's something wrong when people go an about how good everything is.

SALLY: *I* think things are good. I've never had the chance of a good job before. They always said I was stupid at school, always dreaming. When I left, they found out I was epileptic and gave me pills.

SUSAN (IGNORING THE INTERRUPTION): I mean, I couldn't live with my husband if I didn't respect him.

34

FRANKIE: What's he do? Drama teacher, was it? Well, one fine day they'll be doing Romeo and Juliet and he'll be staying late for a few wherefore-art-thous with some budding Vanessa Redgrave...

SUSAN: Rubbish!

SANDRA: The second time I tried to kill myself, I cut my wrists. I've still got the scars. Do you want to see?

PAT (TO NO-ONE IN PARTICULAR): I do think this talk has got very personal. I don't like it when talk gets personal.

LIZ (BREAKING THE SPELL): Well, I'm getting on with some homework while we've got a minute. I don't want to be up till midnight again tonight. My boyfriend has to be up early for his milkround.

SUSAN (LOOKING AT HER WATCH): Oh gosh, I've got to run. I'm going early today. I'm seeing my optician. I've asked Mrs Baslow and she says it's allright. (SHE PICKS UP HER COAT AND HANDBAG)

FRANKIE (AS THE OTHERS GO BACK TO THEIR BOOKS): You *are* a good little girl.

SUSAN (FIRMLY, TO THE CLASS): And I'm definitely going to complain about the heating!

THE CURTAIN CLOSES BEHIND HER AS SHE
COMES TO FRONT OF STAGE AND
ADDRESSES THE AUDIENCE NERVOUSLY

SUSAN: And I *will* complain, you'll see. I'm quite an
assertive person, though I know I don't look it. I was
all set on being an actress when I was younger. I just
loved the theatre. Everybody said I had the looks. I
mean, boyfriends and people like that. Oh, I know
my nose is a bit long and my legs are a little bit short,
but I think little flaws make people interesting. In the
end though, when I got my A levels and looked
around, it seemed like a good idea to be a librarian.
Because I loved books too. (PAUSE) Anyway, it was
a love of the theatre that brought Alec and me
together when we were students. So it was all
worthwhile. And one of the good things about all this
typewriting is that it's something to talk to Alec about.
It's quite interesting, meeting all these new people and
doing new things. Oh, I know what you're thinking:
that awful Frankie woman who smokes! And that silly
Pat going on about the magic of marriage. But it's
good fun really. It *is*. I've done lots of things in the
past few years, and they've all been fun. I've done
watercolour classes, pottery classes, embroidery... I've
even done upholstery, but upholstery is very
demanding physically. I had to give that one up. I
can't honestly say I could mend your settee so you'd
better not ask me. Though I can do some nice
landscapes and vases... but it's just a hobby. That's
why this typing thing is different - because it can lead
to something. And, as I said, it's something to talk to
Alec about. All those characters! That Mrs Baslow!
Honestly! All those beads and bracelets and wearing
her glasses round her neck. (PAUSE) Alec's very

good at listening. *I* am too. I do the listening when he's had a hard day lecturing on Restoration Comedy. (PAUSE) I tend to suspect people who go on about their marriages, don't you? But you don't have to take my word for it. You can come round and see for yourself. After I've seen my optician. You'll be very welcome.

SHE EXITS STAGE LEFT

Scene 5

MUSIC: *NINE TO FIVE* BY SHEENA EASTON. THEN THE CURTAIN GOES UP ON SUSAN'S FRONT ROOM. A DESK AT BACK STAGE CENTRE IS COVERED IN HOMEWORK BOOKS, ALL OF THEM OPEN. THERE ARE TWO ARMCHAIRS FRONT STAGE LEFT AND FRONT STAGE RIGHT SO THE ROOM REFLECTS THE LAYOUT OF FRANKIE'S ROOM BUT LOOKS MORE EXPENSIVE. MUSIC DIES. WE HEAR THE FLUSH OF THE LAVATORY AND SUSAN COMES IN STAGE LEFT, PULLING UP THE JEANS SHE HAS NOW CHANGED INTO. SHE SEATS HERSELF AT THE DESK AND CONTINUES THE HOMEWORK. SHE IS OBVIOUSLY HAVING DIFFICULTY, LOOKING UP EVERY OTHER WORD IN THE SHORTHAND DICTIONARY AND MUTTERING TO HERSELF. ENTER STAGE RIGHT ALEC, WHO CARRIES TWO EARTHENWARE COFFEE MUGS

ALEC: Here. I heard you go to the toilet. I reckoned you were ready for a break. Refreshment for the weary.

SUSAN: Fantastic! I *will* have a break then, just a little one. Give us a chance to have a cuddle. (HUGS HIM)

ALEC (STILL WITH MUGS IN HAND): Careful. I don't want to get scalded.

THEY GO TO FRONT CENTRE STAGE WHERE THEY SIT ON TWO POUFFES IN FRONT OF THE ARMCHAIRS. SUSAN TAKES ONE OF THE MUGS.

ALEC: I'll put on some Vivaldi. (HE MIMES PUTTING A TAPE ON TO A PLAYER. WE HEAR THE START OF VIVALDI'S *FOUR SEASONS*.) Well, how goes it? Pretty boring?

SUSAN: No, not really. Not bad. I'm just tired. I'll have to take out my lenses in a minute.

ALEC: Tell me again - what did the optician say?

SUSAN: He says it's nothing. He says I'm tired, that's all. I think it's the repetition.

ALEC: But it can't be exactly demanding. Intellectually, I mean.

SUSAN (TOO QUICKLY): Oh, it's not. But I don't let on to the others. They'd think I was acting superior.

ALED: You *are* superior. I don't suppose you've told them about the degree.

SUSAN: You're joking! If they knew that, they'd say I was a brainbox. That's what they call Liz - she's a French teacher.

ALEC: Well, it was all your idea. Worth doing, you said.

SUSAN: Oh yes. I'm sure it is. The discipline is good for me. It's six years since...

ALEC: Since you had a job. I know.

SUSAN: And it's not for want of trying.

ALEC: Look, I'm not criticising. You're far too sensitive about it. As far as I'm concerned, you certainly haven't wasted your time. You kept busy, did the right things. I'm proud of you for it. Just because you've not been earning...

SUSAN: But I *am* earning now. At least it'll pay to have the studio redecorated.

ALEC: Studio? Oh...

SUSAN: Yes, I know it's pretentious. But then, *I'm* a pretentious person, aren't I? It's where I'll be doing all my watercolours. I don't want it to go on looking like...

ALEC: ...a nursery.

SUSAN: ...a spare room. I'm not bitter, you know. I know what you say is right - I've managed to do some really good things. Like the art classes. And the Open University. What a world! Upper second in humanities. Fellow of the Library Association. Eight years experience supervising junior staff. And I'm unemployable.

ALEC: Blame Mrs Thatcher. Blame the world economic situation. Why let it bother you? People are important for what they are as human beings, not as economic units.

SUSAN: I wouldn't mind being a successful economic unit right now. As it is, it seems the only chance I've got of ever getting back to work is typing invoices and menu cards and hoping it leads to something better.

ALEC: Like what?

SUSAN: Secretary to someone, I suppose. Someone important, someone who can teach me. (GRIMACES) Some *man*, I suppose.

ALEC: Teach you what?

SUSAN: About... I don't know. Management, organisation, the way things work. *Real* things. I've never been able to grasp how things actually get done in this world. It's always been a mystery to me. Like electricity.

ALEC: If it's any consolation, I've no idea myself how electricity works.

SUSAN: Tell me something. If I left you, would you live on toast?

ALEC: What a strange thing to say. Of course not. I'd go down to the college. (HE SMILES, SO SHE KNOWS IT'S A JOKE) You can get a three course meal for a pound.

SUSAN (HESITANTLY): Look, about this course... What I thought I'd do... I thought this was pretty clever. I thought I'd get a typing job with the council. You know how thin on the ground library jobs are. They only advertise them internally, you see. And if I'm actually working for the council, I'd get the vacancy lists and then I could apply.

ALEC: Perhaps... yes, I'm sure you could. (PAUSE) Look, I thought we might go to that new Woody Allen film tomorrow night. Barry Norman said it wasn't as good as *Annie Hall* but it represented a new direction in Allen's work.

SUSAN (SIGHS): Not tomorrow, love. We've got the test on Friday and tomorrow night I'll have to revise. What about the weekend?

ALEC: I've got a play reading on Friday evening and on Saturday it's the SDP management committee. That's a shame. I should have thought of it earlier.

SUSAN: You go, love. There's no point both of us being miserable.

ALEC: No, no. I'll keep you company, keep the coffee coming in.

SUSAN: You *are* good. What's the reading for? Not *Romeo and Juliet*?

ALEC: No, it's not our term for Shakespeare. Why did you think it was *Romeo and Juliet*?

SUSAN: Oh, some silly reason.

ALEC: It's *A Streetcar Named Desire*.

SUSAN (LAUGHING): Oh God. (BEAT) Look - next week I'll be organised, you'll see. I'll have all my work done early and we'll go out. I promise. (PRESSES AGAINST HIM) I just need to... to do better than the rest of them. This one with the trousers, the one who got told off, she's a hard-faced cow. I'll damn well do better than her. Than *she*.

ALEC: Of course you will.

HE TAKES HER CUP AND HIS OWN AND THEY STAND UP AND MOVE FORWARD. THE CURTAINS CLOSE BEHIND THEM.

ALEC: Look, do you really have to do more work tonight? If the optician said your eyes were getting tired, maybe you should take it seriously. Why don't you take your lenses out now? Really give your eyes a rest?

SUSAN: (CLINGING AFFECTIONATELY TO HIM): Oh, you're right! Damn the jolly gardener! (SHE HUGS HIM AND KICKS OFF HER SLIPPERS) Bugger the smallest tribe in Kenya!

SHE UNBUTTONS HER BLOUSE, THEY
STUMBLE OFF STAGE LEFT, KISSING, HIM
STILL HOLDING THE CUPS. AFTER HALF A
MINUTE, SHE RETURNS, HER CLOTHES IN
DISARRAY, LOOKING SHEEPISH, AND PICKS
UP THE SLIPPERS

SUSAN (TO THE AUDIENCE): Sorry about that.
I'm very embarrassed. I'd forgotten you were here.
And if I leave these lying around (INDICATES
SLIPPERS) I'll never find them without my lenses.
Anyway, don't mind us. You can take ten minutes
off. Go on. Have a beer. Or a coffee. I couldn't get
through the day without my coffee. Only not from the
machine, of course. I only drink *real* coffee and that
machine coffee isn't real at all. I'll probably complain
about it when I complain about the heating. And I *will*
complain about the heating. You'll see.

SHE RUNS OFFSTAGE LEFT. MUSIC: *SEXUAL
HEALING* BY MARVIN GAYE.

END OF ACT ONE

ACT TWO

Scene 1

MUSIC: *THE TIDE IS HIGH* BY BLONDIE. THEN
CURTAIN GOES UP ON THE CLASSROOM. THE
GIRLS SIT AT THEIR DESKS TYPING, BUT
SUSAN, ANN AND SALLY ARE MISSING FROM
THEIR PLACES. THERE ARE CHRISTMAS
TRIMMINGS UP, AND THE GIRLS ALL WEAR
THEIR COATS. MUSIC DIES. ENTER SUSAN,
STAGE LEFT, LOOKING EMBARRASSED. SHE
SLIPS INTO HER PLACE, ALSO STILL IN HER
COAT. THE GIRLS GO THROUGH THE TYPING
MOTIONS ONCE AGAIN.

SUSAN: The good secretary does not always have her
coat on. She should not arrive late nor go home until
all replies are in the post...

FRANKIE: During the first year that Mr Wordsworth
and I were neighbours, our conversation turned to the
cardinal points of poetry...

JENNY: No matter what the political climate,
freedom of speech is an important issue…

PAT: In respect of wild elephants, nature has surely
shown considerable enterprise…

SANDRA: Misfortune mocks mere optimism but may
make for much meditation…

LIZ: In the mollusc kingdom there are myriad
examples of mass migration…

SUSAN: Any attempt to describe the pattern of life in the Isle of Man today must have regard to what is permanent in the environment and what is in the process of change...

LIZ: Silk worms are a lowly form of life but provide us with luxury...

SUSAN: Silk is several times smoother than Harris Tweed...

FRANKIE: Taking the rough with the smooth is one of life's lessons...

JENNY: We are all of us learners in life's vast classroom...

PAT: Everybody learns to make the best of things...

SANDRA: Things fall apart, the centre cannot hold...

FRANKIE: Maureen insists her silk dress is six inches short. She always seems to see faults in frocks...

SUSAN: David and Donald are very good friends. In their young days they lived in poor circumstance and learned to make do and mend...

FRANKIE (INTERRUPTING): They ought to meet Maureen.

SUSAN (IGNORING HER): Skilled in handiwork, they made snaddles. *Saddles, saddles, saddles!* They made saddles and sundry wooden goods and decided to adopt this as their trade...

FRANKIE (STOPS TYPING): What's this place got in common with Russia then?

LIZ: The cold?

FRANKIE: As *well* as the cold. No? Well, people disappear (INDICATES EMPTY SEATS) and nobody says a word.

SUSAN: I thought Ann had got flu.

FRANKIE: Flew away, more like.

PAT: She was having trouble at home. I tried to get her to see it wasn't worth the worry. Don't let it get you down, I said.

SUSAN: What sort of trouble?

PAT: Her little boy. His hair started falling out in handfulls. She blamed herself, not being there. Well, her mother doesn't seem much use in looking after kids. But he's got to be without you *some* time, I said...

SUSAN: Not at 18 months.

JENNY (RESUMES TYPING): Far from the fir forests, flocks of falcons flew over our farm...

PAT: Disasters of dire proportion destroyed the dominant dinosaur...

SANDRA: O bee, where is thy sting? O viper, where is thy venom?

SUSAN: The Saharan subspecies of sand snake shows some susceptibility to the sun...

LIZ: But the Bavarian butter bat builds nests in bare basements by and large...

FRANKIE: It hangs upside down in deep darkness...

JENNY: It flits and flies fortuitously as dusk turns dimmer...

PAT: She asked for help. The other one. She asked Mrs Baslow.

LIZ (STOPS TYPING): Who?

PAT: The other one. Sally. The one who was dyslexic or epileptic or something. She said she was falling behind. *You can only do your best*, I said. I think Mrs Baslow gave her extra homework.

FRANKIE: That would be a lot of help. Bugger! This space bar's stuck. I can't get it right.

LIZ: These are rotten machines. The lock's gone on mine and I have to hold it down when I do a line of capitals.

FRANKIE: Well, I'm not having this. It's only five weeks to the exam.

SUSAN: Oh God! Is it really?

PAT: I'm sure we'll all do better than we think.

MRS BASLOW (ENTERING STAGE LEFT): Hello, everyone. Just carry on working.

FRANKIE: Excuse me, Mrs Baslow. My space bar's gone funny. Can you have a look at it?

MRS BASLOW: Well, I'm sure it can't be anything serious. They've all just been serviced, you know. Are you sure you haven't been doing something you shouldn't?

FRANKIE: With a typewriter? It's not the right shape.

LIZ: My lock is broken, Mrs Baslow.

SUSAN: And my backspace is a bit temperamental, actually.

FRANKIE (CONTEMPTUOUSLY TO SUSAN): Temperamental, is it? Give it a smack then.

SUSAN: When I do corrections, they don't come on the line.

MRS BASLOW (TO REST OF CLASS): I take it you other girls are fine.

PAT: Oh yes, Mrs Baslow, just fine.

MRS BASLOW: It's terribly expensive, of course, mending typewriters. Which is why we must take proper care of them. And remember - when you go on your first job, you'll probably have to use a typewriter that's not exactly in the peak of condition. Typists have to (BEAT) be adaptable.

FRANKIE: But it's only five weeks to the exam...

MRS BASLOW: And you've got so much to learn before then. Tabulation, menus, programmes... Wait a minute. (TRYING IT OUT) This space bar is working fine. It goes down allright. You just have to... well, you have to pull a bit when you want it up again.

FRANKIE: There's always *something* that reminds me of our Des... Well, I'm sorry, Mrs B, but I can't work with a faulty machine. Not with the exam so near.

MRS BASLOW (ANNOYED): It's a shame you didn't complain sooner, you know.

FRANKIE: It only just happened.

MRS BASLOW: As I said. Something you were doing, perhaps.

FRANKIE: Yes. I was *typing*.

JENNY: Perhaps Frankie could have one of the spare machines, Mrs Baslow. If Sally and Ann aren't coming back...

MRS BASLOW (RELIEVED): Yes. And *you* have the other one, Elizabeth. What a good idea! And (TO SUSAN) that just leaves you, my dear. This sort of

49

thing, looking at typewriters, does take up so much time, you know, when there's so much more work to be done...

SUSAN: I'm sorry, Mrs Baslow. I don't want to be a trouble. It's just that...

MRS BASLOW: I'll see if we can get you another machine very soon. In the meantime... well, if your corrections don't come on the line, you'll just have to make fewer errors. It will be a good discipline for you.

SUSAN (DEFEATED): Yes, Mrs Baslow.

MRS BASLOW (TRIUMPHANT, TO CLASS AS A WHOLE): Right. Now here's something to cheer you up. I'm going to let you all out half an hour early because it's the last day of term. Well, it's not quite the last day of term, not officially. But I'm sure you'll all want time for your Christmas shopping, so I'm proposing to finish a day early. (THERE IS SURPRISED MURMURING IN THE GROUP) And don't forget you've all got work to hand in on the first day of next term. So Merry Christmas to you all!

MRS BASLOW EXITS STAGE LEFT AS THE OTHERS RESPOND WITH A RAGGED *MERRY CHRISTMAS, MRS BASLOW*. THEN THEY ALL GET UP AND MILL ABOUT

PAT: I was *hoping* to get on to tabulation and menus before the holiday.

LIZ: Well, I think it's a good job we're off early. I can get Barry's tea and we can go to the pub for once. And I could *do* with extra time for shopping.

PAT: *I* think that's a rather negative attitude, Liz, and I'm surprised to hear a teacher say a thing like that.

JENNY: Well. That's that then. Anyway, I'm off. Merry Christmas! (EXIT STAGE LEFT)

LIZ: Wait for me! Merry Christmas, everybody! (FOLLOWS JENNY)

SANDRA (CALLING AFTER HER): More people kill themselves at Christmas than at any other time.

PAT (MUSING): I'm disappointed in Liz. I'm disappointed in Mrs Baslow, come to that. I've got a lot of time for Mrs Baslow normally. She's very *professional*. This whole place is very professional, if you ask *me*. But I don't think it's right we should take time off.

FRANKIE: Professional? It's *criminal.* That's the only kind of *professional* it is. I wonder how much the government pays that old bat to keep us off the streets?

SUSAN: Alec won't be expecting me, that's the trouble, and I don't want to get in his way. He's got lots of essays to mark on John Osborne and working class influences in the theatre.

FRANKIE: Thank God our Des is a truck driver. At least it's something he can't do at home.

PAT: People talk about home and getting home early but what's the point of having a nice home if you're going to be there all day getting it untidy? Personally, I like to be out of mine. I like meeting people. All sorts of people. (TO SANDRA) Do *you* like meeting people?

SANDRA: Not really. Not *most* people.

FRANKIE: OK. That's it. On that cheery note, I'm off. (SHE EXITS STAGE LEFT IN A HURRY)

SUSAN (SHOUTING AFTER HER): Well, Merry Christmas (IGNORED, SHE TURNS TO THE OTHERS) Merry Christmas then. (SHE WANDERS OFF STAGE LEFT DISCONSOLATELY)

PAT (TO SANDRA): You say you don't like meeting people. But you like meeting *me*, don't you? And being here must be better than that hostel you keep going on about.

SANDRA: I *don't* keep going on about it.

PAT: But you've told me...

SANDRA: You keep asking, that's all. You keep asking so I tell you. But I *don't* go on about it. I don't talk about it at all to anyone else. I don't like to talk about it because I don't like to *think* about it.

PAT: You've told me about the warden and what a terrible person you think she is...

SANDRA: She's a bitch. And a cow.

PAT: Well, I prefer not to use words like that. I'm
sure she's only doing her job. I'm sure the only reason
she stops you smoking is so you won't set the bed
alight. And the other girls...

SANDRA: They're *all* bitches. And cows.

PAT: Well, I've already said what I think of words
like that. But just because they borrow your clothes...

SANDRA: They stole my knickers. They waited till I
washed them first.

PAT: Well, you can't be sure of that. We all lose
small articles of underclothing now and again...
Anyway, it only serves to indicate to me that you
must be glad to leave that place to come here. It gets
you out of yourself. Getting yourself out of yourself is
one of the most important things in life. It helps you
get other people out of *themselves.* You know, that's
one thing I'm good at. I think that's why Arthur
married me. Because - I'll tell you something - he
wasn't very good at it himself. I mean, he's so shy.
The things I had to do to get him to ask me out in the
first place... well, nothing improper of course, nothing
you wouldn't want your friends to know about. No, I
don't mean that sort of thing. But you have to make
the effort with people sometimes, don't you?

SANDRA: Why?

PAT: Why? Why? Because otherwise life isn't worth
living. You've got to do your best. Who was it who

said the life of Man today must have regard to what is permanent in the environment and what is in the process of change? I just can't remember at the moment. God put us on this earth to help each other just like I help you. That's how we find a better life.

SANDRA: There's no such thing as a better life. Life's all the same. Life is just yourself. And you can't change yourself.

PAT: Of course you can change yourself - that's what we've all come here for. What a strange person you are. I hope you don't mind me saying that. Come on and I'll get you a coffee out of the machine and we can drink it in the lift going down. And we can talk about what we're doing for Christmas. After all, we won't be seeing each other till next term. (AS THEY EXIT STAGE LEFT) Do you know what Mrs Baslow asked me? She said: *What's the one thing in life that's more wonderful than teaching?* And, you know, I couldn't answer. And you know what the answer was? Go on, have a think. It's easy really...(HER VOICE FADES AWAY AS SHE WALKS OFFSTAGE LEFT)

SANDRA (REMAINING BEHIND AND FACING THE AUDIENCE): She didn't ask me to have Christmas Dinner with her. I thought she was going to, but she didn't. I suppose she knew I wouldn't want to. She knew I'd say no. I would too. I *would* say no. (SHOUTING AFTER PAT) It's learning, isn't it? That's the one thing that's better than teaching. I'm right, aren't I? (TO AUDIENCE) I thought *everybody* knew that. (FOLLOWS PAT DISCONSOLATELY OFF STAGE LEFT AS CURTAIN FALLS.)

Scene 2:

MUSIC: *LITTLE DRUMMER BOY* BY BING CROSBY AND DAVID BOWIE IN FRONT OF CURTAINS. TRAFFIC NOISE AND FALLING SNOW EFFECT WITH LIGHTS INDICATE IT IS A STREET SCENE. MUSIC DIES. ENTER STAGE RIGHT CAROLINE, OBVIOUSLY LOOKING FOR SOMEONE. ENTER STAGE LEFT PAT, CARRYING SHOPPING BAGS AND CLUTCHING A SHOPPING LIST. SHE SEES CAROLINE AND MAKES STRAIGHT FOR HER.

PAT: Excuse me. I could see you looking worried. Are you a stranger here? Are you lost? Are you looking for something?

CAROLINE (STARTLED): No, that's OK. I was looking for *someone*. He's not turned up.

PAT: Because if you're a stranger I can probably direct you. I know the town quite well although they've changed a lot of it in the past few years.

CAROLINE: No. Really…

PAT: Yes, they have. If you'd lived here as long as I have, you'd realise. A lot of very nice buildings have come down and the roads are much wider now. Still, I suppose that's progress. You can't stand in the way of progress, that's what I always say.

CAROLINE: No, I'm not lost. I was looking for someone. I'm sure he'll get here eventually. It's very crowded.

PAT: But my husband Arthur says: *Progress does not always mean going forward.* And I think *he's* right too.

CAROLINE (DECIDING ON A RETREAT): I know. I'll go for a coffee and come back later. Thanks for your help. (EXITS IN A RUSH, STAGE LEFT)

PAT: Strange girl. I hope she finds her way. And of course, it's crowded. It's Christmas. And you always get bigger crowds if you make the roads wider.

SHE EXITS STAGE RIGHT

THEN: ENTER STAGE LEFT FRANKIE AND DES. BOTH ARE IN OVERCOATS, SCARVES AND GLOVES. FRANKIE, IN A DIFFERENT OVERCOAT FROM HER PREVIOUS APPEARANCE, CARRIES SHOPPING BAGS.

FRANKIE: Same plan as last year then?

DES: What's that?

FRANKIE: Anything we want over four pounds ninety-nine, I pick it up and run and you threaten the shop staff, stop 'em from chasing after me.

DES: Aw, very amusing!

FRANKIE: OK, *you* pick it up and run and *I'll* threaten the staff. I don't mind swopping roles. I'm a modern woman, that's me.

DES: You don't have to make out we're badly off. We're not. And you don't have to make out I'm mean or something. I don't mind lashing out with a bit of cash at Christmas. I've got bonuses coming, I have. It's just that…

FRANKIE: Just what?

DES: Just that you always take too bloody long choosing things. I mean, with women, shopping is so bloody important, isn't it? It's like sport is with men. You get women today that are just shopping *fans*. Their whole lives revolve round it.

FRANKIE: I know what you mean. Gangs of women fighting in the streets, pulling up paving stones. (SHOUTS LIKE NEWSPAPER SELLER) Rival shoppers in terror clash. Read all about it! (SHOUTS LIKE FOOTBALL HOOLIGAN) *Marks and Sparks rule OK, British Home Stores are shit. Boots the Chemist - easy, easy, easy!* (RESUMES NORMAL VOICE) It's a wonder I didn't see it all before.

DES: Oh, you can mock, but you know I'm right. It's a modern mark of the sickness of the consumer society. Women go funny in the head when they get into a big store. It's an illness, an addiction, like drugs or drink.

FRANKIE: You didn't have to come with me, you know. You could have just said: *Frankie, I don't want to come Christmas shopping*. I'd have hit you with our Darren's baseball bat, but at least I'd've respected you.

DES: That's not it. That's not it at all. I just think it's actually very silly for us both to go shopping together. After all, we're buying *each other* presents so we'll want to keep it a surprise.

FRANKIE: Surprise? Oh no, not another pair of black lace crotchless French knickers with red bows? Not another set of exotic fishnet tights with matching see-through bra? You talk about the time I take shopping - it's nothing to the time I take carting stuff back and having innocent shopgirls catch a shocking glimpse of the sad man I married. (PAUSE) Allright then. I'll see you back here in an hour.

DES (BRIGHTENING): Oh, good!

FRANKIE: Only don't have too much.

DES: What do you mean?

FRANKIE: I mean it's still too early for a merry Christmas. Go on - get on with it.

DES: See you. (EXITS STAGE LEFT)

FRANKIE: See you. (SHE EXITS STAGE RIGHT)

LIZ ENTERS STAGE LEFT AND STANDS IN MIDDLE OF STAGE, LOOKING ABOUT HER. SANDRA, ALSO IN OVERCOAT, THEN ENTERS STAGE RIGHT

LIZ (SEEING SANDRA): Hello there. Hello, Sandra. Fancy seeing you.

SANDRA: Nobody *does*. Nobody fancies seeing *me*. There's never anybody who wants to see *me*. Not for a proper reason anyway. Sometimes people follow me but that's because they don't like me. What are *you* doing here? Have *you* been following me?

LIZ: Now why should I follow you? Anyway, I was here first.

SANDRA: There's more than one way of following a person. One way of following a person is to get in front of that person and let that person follow you.

LIZ: Or you could just stand still and wait for the world to go round and in the end you're bound to see everybody you've ever known.

SANDRA (SUSPICIOUS): That's stupid, that is. I've never heard anything so stupid. I don't believe that could ever happen.

LIZ (EXASPERATED): I think you're right. I'm supposed to meet Barry here and I'm half an hour late as it is. Maybe he's been and gone. Maybe he's following me by going home and waiting for me to go home too.

SANDRA: You think I'm stupid.

LIZ: No. Really. I *don't* think you're stupid. I just think I better go back now and see if Barry's gone home. That's probably what he's done, now that I think about it. Couldn't be bothered to wait for me.

SANDRA: What if he comes when you've gone? Shall I tell him what you said?

LIZ: But you won't know him. You don't know what he looks like.

SANDRA: You could tell me what he looks like.

LIZ (EVASIVE): Well, he's just *ordinary*. I don't think I could describe him really.

SANDRA: You said he was a milkman. You *did*. I remember. I know what a milkman looks like.

LIZ: Well, he'll not be carrying his milk crate. He'll be off duty. In plain clothes.

SANDRA: I'll look out. I'll look out for him.

LIZ: Haven't you got anything better to do?

SANDRA: No. Not really. They don't like us stopping in during the day. They don't like *me* stopping in.

LIZ: Well, it's better than them not letting you *out*. (PAUSE) It's been very nice, Sandra, very nice meeting you like this. But I better be going. Merry Christmas if I don't bump into you again before the big day. Merry Christmas. (EXITS STAGE LEFT)

SANDRA (TO AUDIENCE): I've not tried to kill myself for two months now. The warden said that was very good. She said it showed I was trying. But I don't like to be out of practice.

ALEC IN OVERCOAT ENTERS STAGE LEFT, LOOKS ROUND NERVOUSLY, WALKS TO RIGHT OF STAGE, ALL THE TIME ON THE LOOKOUT FOR SOMETHING. HE PULLS THE COAT COLLAR UP.

SANDRA (GOING OVER TO HIM): Are you a milkman?

ALEC (SURPRISED): Sorry?

SANDRA: I said are you a milkman?

ALEC: No. Sorry. There's a supermarket round the corner.

SANDRA: I don't go into supermarkets. People watch you. Store detectives. They watch you. They follow you.

ALEC (ALARMED): Er... that must be worrying.

SANDRA: Not if you don't go in supermarkets. I never do.

SANDRA EXITS STAGE LEFT, A RELIEVED ALEC STARTS TO GAZE AROUND AS THOUGH LOOKING FOR SOMEONE.

ENTER STAGE RIGHT FRANKIE. SHE IS CARRYING TWO LARGE SHOPPING BAGS FULL OF PARCELS. SHE WALKS PAST ALEC AND STANDS AT LEFT OF STAGE, ALSO ON

THE LOOKOUT. AFTER A SHORT TIME,
CAROLINE ENTERS STAGE LEFT, LOOKS
ROUND, SEES ALEC, RUSHES PAST FRANKIE
AND UP TO ALEC AND KISSES HIM
PASSIONATELY. FRANKIE REGISTERS THIS
BUT WITHOUT GREAT INTEREST AND
RETURNS TO LOOKING FOR SOMEONE. THE
SNOW EFFECT DIES AWAY.

ALEC (BREAKING AWAY FROM CAROLINE):
Caroline! I told you not to come. You can't do this
sort of thing in the street.

CAROLINE: You're so silly, Alec. You're such a
worrier. Why are older people such worriers? (SHE
KISSES HIM PASSIONATELY AGAIN. FRANKIE
REGISTERS THIS BUT AGAIN TAKES LITTLE
INTEREST.)

ALEC (PUSHING CAROLINE AWAY AGAIN):
There's no sane reason for you to be here.

CAROLINE: I had to give you your Christmas
present. Here it is! (SHE TAKES A SMALL
CHRISTMAS PARCEL OUT OF THE SHOPPING
BAG SHE IS CARRYING) Aren't you going to open
it?

ALEC: I am *not* going to open it. Not now. (HE
STUFFS THE PARCEL IN HIS OVERCOAT
POCKET AND CONTINUES TO LOOK ROUND
NERVOUSLY) I told you she was going to be here.

CAROLINE: But she's not here yet.

ALEC: She'll be here soon. We're finishing off our shopping. We always do the Christmas shopping together.

CAROLINE: That's nice. I think married people should share everything. Well, *almost* everything. You haven't asked me what it is. Your present. You haven't asked.

ALEC: Allright, what is it?

CAROLINE: It's boxer shorts. They're very fashionable now. A lot more fashionable than your old Y-fronts. I've bought you a pair with a Union Jack. I think it's important to be patriotic, don't you?

ALEC: No, I don't.

CAROLINE: I don't suppose *she* does either. But I want to meet her, you see. I want to know what she's like.

ALEC: You're mad.

CAROLINE: No, I'm not. I'm curious. When you sleep with a man, you become very curious about his wife. You think: she must be a lot like me because she has the same taste in things.

ALEC: She doesn't buy me Union Jack underpants.

CAROLINE: Boxer shorts. No. Well, it's the age gap.

ALEC: OK. You've given me my Christmas present. Now go.

CAROLINE: Haven't you bought anything for me?

ALEC: No, I have not.

CAROLINE (LAUGHING): How selfish men are!
Especially older men. Especially older *married* men.
(HER TONE CHANGES) Oh, don't look so worried.
I won't give you away.

ALEC: What if she'd seen you, just then? What if
she'd seen us...?

CAROLINE: Kissing? Well, it's a theatrical thing,
isn't it? All theatrical people kiss each other. Anyway,
she isn't here and she didn't see us.

ALEC: If she comes along now, what am I supposed
to say?

CAROLINE: Tell her the truth. I mean, the part of it
you can afford to tell her. You're my tutor and I'm
playing Blanche DuBois in *A Streetcar Named
Desire*.

ALEC: And we just happened to meet in the street!

CAROLINE: Why not? People do. (SHE LOOKS
OFFSTAGE RIGHT) Is this her? I bet it is. She looks
your type.

ALEC (ALSO LOOKING OFFSTAGE RIGHT): Oh
God! (HE WAVES)

SUSAN ENTERS STAGE RIGHT, CARRYING
FOUR SHOPPING BAGS AND WEARING A
DIFFERENT OVERCOAT FROM HER LAST
APPEARANCE

SUSAN: Alec! (SHE HESITATES AS SHE SEES
CAROLINE)

ALEC: Sue! Susan! (BEAT) Ah, Susan. Meet
Caroline. She's one of my students. Caroline, this is
Susan. My wife.

SUSAN (OFFERS HER HAND TO CAROLINE):
Hello.

CAROLINE (TAKING HER HAND): Hi. Alec is a
really great teacher. I've really come on a lot since
I've known him.

SUSAN: Yes, he is. I'm very proud of him.

ALEC (WRETCHED): We just met in the street.

CAROLINE: I'm glad we did. It gives me chance to
say Merry Christmas.

ALEC: Yes. Right. Merry Christmas.

CAROLINE: But I've got to be off now. Merry
Christmas. Merry Christmas, Mrs Constable. (SHE
WAVES TO THEM BOTH AND EXITS STAGE
RIGHT)

ALEC: It's funny how you meet people in the street.

SUSAN (SHE HAS CAUGHT SIGHT OF FRANKIE
WHO IS GAZING IN THE OPPOSITE
DIRECTION): Oh no!

ALEC: What is it?

SUSAN: I can't stand it!

ALEC: Oh God! It's not what you think!

SUSAN: Yes, it is!

ALEC (GUILTILY): No, it's not!

SUSAN: Yes, it is! it's her! *She*. She's here.

ALEC: Who? (LOOKS ROUND)

SUSAN: That dreadful Frankie woman. I don't think
she's seen me. I don't... (AT THIS POINT FRANKIE
LOOKS ACROSS AND SUSAN WAVES)
Ahhh....Hello, hello there!

FRANKIE (STARTLED): Hello then.

SUSAN (MOVING ACROSS TO FRANKIE, WITH
ALEC IN TOW): Hello, Frankie. What are you doing
here? Have you been shopping? (REGISTERS THE
PARCELS) Oh yes, you've been shopping. I can see.
Alec, this is Frankie, who's on the course with me.
Frankie, this is Alec, my husband.

FRANKIE (TAKEN ABACK): Oooohhh. I mean
hello. So you're...

ALEC (DESPERATELY, REALIZING HE'S BEEN SEEN): Alec. Frankie - that must be short for Frances.

FRANKIE: No, it isn't actually. A lot of people make that mistake. It's short for Francesca. My mother was Italian.

ALEC (AWKWARDLY): How interesting. (LAMELY) That your mother was Italian.

FRANKIE: So it *is* shorter. Frankie *is* shorter than Francesca. But it's not shorter than Frances.

ALEC: No. Right. It's not.

SUSAN: And you've been shopping. We're doing *our* shopping actually.

FRANKIE: I guessed you'd like to do your shopping together. Des and I like to do it separately. Well, he doesn't like to do it at all. He comes out with me and goes to the pub. But he helps me carry the parcels home.

DES (ENTERING STAGE LEFT): Ey up!

FRANKIE: Speak of the devil. Ello, Des. Come and meet some people I know. This is Susan who's on the course with me...

DES (CLEARLY RECOGNISING THE NAME): Oh, you mean... Ello, Susan.

FRANKIE: And Alec...

SUSAN: My husband.

DES: Ello.

FRANKIE: And this is Des.

DES: I reckon she'll have mentioned me.

SUSAN: She talks about you a lot.

DES: I thought she might.

FRANKIE: Come on, Des. We've got a bus to catch.

ALEC (QUIETLY FRANTIC): Must you go? I mean, maybe we could have a drink somewhere...

DES: Ay, that sounds a good idea.

SUSAN: But we *do* have a lot of shopping, Alec.

ALEC: But we could manage one drink. Have a chat. A chance to get to know each other... (TO FRANKIE IN LOWERED TONE) to explain things...You know...

FRANKIE: Fraid not. Don't want to miss that bus.

DES: We could catch the next one. We could have a drink and catch the next one.

FRANKIE: Darren's at Jean's house and she won't want him stopping late. She's had him twice this week already. Come on, Des. Stop dawdling. Take this and this. (SHE HANDS HIM PARCELS) It's coming on to snow again.

DES (STRETCHES OUT HAND): No, it's not. (PAUSE, THEN HE TAKES PARCELS): Oh. Right. Well. Some other time then.

ALEC: Some other time.

DES: Merry Christmas!

ALEC, FRANKIE and SUSAN in unison: Merry Christmas!

DES (IN LOW VOICE TO FRANKIE): He didn't seem so bad.

FRANKIE: Shut yer mouth.

EXIT FRANKIE AND PROTESTING DES STAGE LEFT

SUSAN: Well, you seem to have taken to them.

ALEC: Yes, they're very nice. Especially the woman. Rather quiet. The sort that keeps her own counsel, I would have thought.

SUSAN: You must be joking. She can't stop yapping. The things I don't know about her and that Des you could write on your fingernail.

ALEC: Oh. Oh dear.

SUSAN: Compared with her, *I'm* the silent type. And you know what a gossip *I* am.

ALEC: No, you're not. You're... eloquent. An interesting storyteller. You're...yes, interesting. The most interesting woman I've ever met. The one *real* woman. The one I *really* love. I mean, whatever else... (HE HUGS HER AWKWARDLY)

SUSAN: Well, thanks. I know you love me but it's nice to be told. (BEAT) What brought this on then, saying all these nice things?

ALEC: Nothing.

SUSAN: It won't get you out of doing the shopping, saying nice things about me. Come on, let's get it over!

ALEC (IN A DAZE): Over. Yes. Over. *All* over, I shouldn't wonder.

HE WALKS WITH LEADEN GAIT AS SHE LEADS HIM BY THE HAND OFFSTAGE RIGHT

Scene 3

MUSIC: *DO YOU KNOW WHERE YOU'RE GOING TO?* BY DIANA ROSS. THEN CURTAIN UP ON THE CLASSROOM. SOME CHRISTMAS DECORATIONS ARE STILL UP, BUT THEY ARE TATTY AND TORN. FRANKIE IS SITTING ALONE, WORKING ON HER SHORTHAND, WEARING HER COAT. MUSIC DIES. ENTER, AFTER A MINUTE OR SO, SUSAN, STAGE

LEFT, WITH COAT AND SHOPPING BAGS. IN
BOTH CASES, THE COATS ARE DIFFERENT
FROM THE ONES THEY WORE IN THE LAST
SCENE.

FRANKIE (LOOKING UP): Well, hello.

SUSAN (OBVIOUSLY NOT PLEASED TO SEE
HER): Hello. I didn't think you'd be in this early.
(BEAT) I thought I'd get in before the class started.
I've got an exercise to finish, a transcription. I should
have done it in the holiday...

FRANKIE: Me too. (PAUSE) Did you have a good
Christmas?

SUSAN (RELUCTANTLY): Well...

FRANKIE: I know. Quiet. It always is without kids.
Our Darren took three days to teach his dad to play
Space Invaders on his digital watch. They don't seem
to want to play cowboys and indians any more. It's
not *bang, bang, you're dead* like it used to be. It's
megaton holocaust or nothing.

SUSAN: I don't like it. Space Invaders *or* cowboy
guns. It's all violence of some sort. And the boys who
play at killing - what sort of men do they grow up
into?

FRANKIE: What sort of men do they grow up into
anyway? That's the difference between you and me,
love. I'm a realist. I'm not always looking to change
things. I suppose I'm quite pleased with what I've got.
I'm pleased with Darren. He's a smashing kid. He'll

grow up all right, violence or no violence, if I don't murder him first. And then there's Des - he's a smashing kid too.

SUSAN: I never know how seriously to take you when you talk about your husband. I must say he seemed very nice.

FRANKIE (LAUGHS): Well, Des isn't perfect. Like I said, you shouldn't always be looking to change things. Sometimes you have to settle for what's available. But he's decent, is Des. He's a good father to Darren and the best man I ever went with. Oh, you should have seen them, some of those idiots I used to have for boyfriends. When they'd be dancing with you, they'd always be singing the words of the record in your ear and you could smell the Newcastle Brown. And it was always *Delilah*. Every man I ever went with wanted to be Tom Jones. The things you put up with when you don't know any better. I've still got the scars... (SHE STARTS TO LIFT HER SWEATER) Well, never mind.

SUSAN (SHOCKED): You mean your boyfriends used to beat you up?

FRANKIE: Yes and no. I'll be honest. It was usually a fair fight. There's some of them still walking round with steel plates in their heads.

SUSAN: Why?

FRANKIE: Why? Because I was angry. I used to get mad. You know how people talk about seeing red? Well, that's the way it was with me. Really. There'd be a red stuff come down over my eyes like the start of a James Bond film. Then I'd lash out.

SUSAN: But why were you angry?

FRANKIE: Because they were men and rubbish men at that, the sort that real men wouldn't give tuppence for. But because they were men, they could go places I couldn't go. They could always earn more money than me for a start, some of them with brains the size of peanuts, just by digging holes in the road. Thank God for Maggie Thatcher! She's shown them they're not God's gift. For the first time in their lives! Oh, that woman's really got her own back!

SUSAN (EVEN MORE SHOCKED): That's a terrible thing to say. Suppose Des lost his job?

FRANKIE: Yeah, you're right. But you've got to see the funny side sometimes. And you've got to hit out to keep from going barmy. I don't actually bash people these days - I do it with words. But it's the same principle. Helps get me through life. And places like this. So I don't end up like our Sandra over there (INDICATES SANDRA'S EMPTY DESK WITH A NOD) putting aspirins in the gin.

SUSAN: Do you think there'll be any hope... of a job?

FRANKIE (TAPS HEAD): Up here, no. (TOUCHES BREAST) Down here, I keep feeling... maybe. And anyway, it's a change from clearing up after men. While it lasts. But you had a good job, didn't you? Once. Why'd you give it up?

73

SUSAN: I got pregnant. It didn't last. I had a miscarriage. But by that time, I'd...

FRANKIE: ...burned your bridges.

SUSAN (SUDDENLY ALARMED): I don't know why I'm telling you these things. You're probably not interested.

FRANKIE: Don't worry. I won't blab your business all over the shop. *I* don't give people away.

SUSAN: You see... I'd been pregnant before. (BEAT) It was when we first started. Before we were married. We should have been more careful. We were very rational about it. We discussed it and came to a joint decision. It was the right thing to do. We *thought* it was. We could never have afforded a baby on student grants. But we didn't know there wouldn't be a second chance. That the second time, when everything was neat and ready, and the third and the fourth... that we'd lose them all. And now... (GLANCES DOWN SUDDENLY AT THE BOOK IN HER HANDS) Oh God, I'm hopeless! I'm not going to get through this exam. Not the shorthand. I stay up till the early hours. I practise, I learn...15, 20 new outlines every night. Next day, it's all gone. It might as well be Egyptian heiroglyphics.

FRANKIE: The mummy's curse. Only in your case...

SUSAN: I'm *not* one. And I never will be. (PAUSE) You may not believe this but I used to be very good at school. I used to come top of the class, win prizes. But here... I can't do it. I can't do any of it. You don't know how humiliating that is. If I'd *got* kids, I'd blame *them* for taking up my time. I only wish Alec wasn't so good about it. He's started darning his own socks now and they fall apart after two days. I've never had more than 40 per cent in any test so far. I hate it. It's so boring. I hate the place. I hate that sanctimonious bitch Mrs Baslow. But you and Pat and Liz, you'll get through. You're OK. You can do it. *I* can't. I'm going to quit. I've decided.

FRANKIE: Rubbish. You'll stick it out. And we'll all get jobs. And in 20 years we'll have a reunion and we'll get drunk on sherry and say how great it was. *All* of us.

SUSAN (A GLIMMER OF HOPE): You really think so?

FRANKIE: I know so. (BEAT) You don't hit out, that's your trouble. You keep it bottled up inside. You want to cause a bit of trouble once in a while, let off a bit of steam...

SUSAN: But I wouldn't know how. It's not me, is it? It's not... Ooohhh!! (SHE SUDDENLY CRIES OUT AND COVERS HER FACE WITH HER HANDS)

FRANKIE (ALARMED): What is it?

SUSAN: My lens has come out. Don't move. Don't come close. If it's not on the desk, it could be on the floor. You have to be careful. They're easy to tread on. (SHE KNEELS DOWN AND STARTS GROPING ABOUT ON THE FLOOR).

ENTER STAGE LEFT MRS BASLOW,
FOLLOWED BY THE REST OF THE CLASS

MRS BASLOW: Right, girls - hurry up please! (THE
GIRLS FIND THEIR SEATS AND GET THEIR
BOOKS OUT ETC) Now, we don't have much time
today. As you know, we're very near the exam and
just to keep you on your toes, I'm going to give you a
surprise typing test. (THERE ARE GENERAL
GROANS AT THIS ANNOUNCEMENT. MRS
BASLOW WALKS DOWN THE AISLE NEXT TO
SUSAN'S DESK WHERE SUSAN IS STILL
FEVERISHLY SEARCHING ON HANDS AND
KNEES. MRS BASLOW SUDDENLY LOOKS
DOWN AT HER FEET) Oh dear, I've trodden on
something.

SUSAN (FRANTIC): No! Oh no!

LIZ: I was hoping to use today for revision, Mrs
Baslow. I was hoping to practise my S stroke.

MRS BASLOW: I'm sure you'll find the test very
useful. I'll start handing out the papers. (SHE GOES
TO HER DESK TO GET THEM)

SUSAN (SLOWLY GETTING TO HER FEET) Mrs
Baslow... Mrs Baslow... (HER VOICE HAS A
DISTANT QUALITY TO IT, A QUALITY OF
SUPPRESSED ANGER AND DESPERATION AND
SHE LOOKS INTO THE MIDDLE DISTANCE,
NOT FOCUSING HER EYES)

MRS BASLOW: What is it, Susan?

SUSAN: You trod... you broke... you....(PAUSE) You haven't replaced my typewriter - the one with the faulty backspace.

MRS BASLOW: There just hasn't been another machine available. We've had such an influx of private students lately.

SUSAN: You... you... (PAUSE) I don't see how I can do this test on a faulty typewriter.

MRS BASLOW (DISMISSIVE): Now, don't be silly. You've managed so far...

SUSAN: And then there's the heating.

MRS BASLOW: What heating?

SUSAN: Exactly. There isn't any. You said we could have the heating on after Christmas. But it's January and there isn't any heating.

MRS BASLOW: But we've had a very mild winter. Everyone has remarked on it. And anyway, many of you will be getting jobs with small firms who are desperately trying to cut down on heating bills and...

SUSAN: And I'd like to be called Mrs Constable. (SHE LOOKS ROUND AT THE REST OF THE CLASS) That's my name. Mrs Constable. That's who I am. (SHE SHOUTS) For God's sake, I'm 36 years old!

MRS BASLOW (COMING TO THE FRONT ROW, SUDDENLY CONCERNED): Are you ill? If you're ill, you can be excused the test. If you're *genuinely* ill...

SUSAN: Ill? I'm not ill.

MRS BASLOW: If it's your time of the month... If you want to go home...

SUSAN (SHE GAZES OUT OVER AUDIENCE AS IF IN A TRANCE AND CALLS OUT IN A SING-SONG VOICE): Ill? Not ill! The jolly girl is in a dreadful rage...

MRS BASLOW: What? What do you mean?

SUSAN: Susan fumes while teacher stares...

MRS BASLOW: Are you having a breakdown? (TO THE OTHERS) Is she having a breakdown?

FRANKIE: I think her backspace has become a bit temperamental.

SUSAN: Susan fails at typing, jibes at sniping (TO THE OTHERS) Shorthand is foolish, learn to paint like Rembrandt. (TO LIZ) French is fairly fancy...

LIZ (AMUSED, TAKING IT UP): French is out of favour, fit only for failing fortune. Touch typing is terrible...

SUSAN: The class is cold and clammy...

FRANKIE (LAUGHS): Dirty dense fog falls on desks and floor alike...

SANDRA (LEAPING TO HER FEET): Speech is sometimes sharp, but razors on the wrist bring rare relief...

PAT (ALARMED) You don't know what you're saying. You don't know what you're playing ...

JENNY (TO SANDRA): Hospitals hallways hate hysterical no-hopers.

SANDRA: Mrs Baslow is a cow and a... and a...

SUSAN: And a bitch and a bitch and a bitch!

MRS BASLOW (ANGRY NOW) Stop it! How dare you!

FRANKIE (TO MRS BASLOW) When a sad lass fails, she goes off the rails...

MRS BASLOW (FURIOUS): Stop it Stop it!!

SUSAN (TO MRS BASLOW): My previous best was 38 out of 83. That was eight weeks ago...

SANDRA: Tatty text books are torn by tormented typists... (SHE STARTS TO TEAR UP THE BOOK ON PAT'S DESK)

PAT: That book is mine, purchased with my precious pounds!

THEY STRUGGLE, PAT GETS THE BOOK OFF
HER, SANDRA RUNS OUT OF THE ROOM,
EXITS STAGE LEFT

SUSAN (SCREAMING NOW): Furious females
smash faulty machines... (HEAVES TYPEWRITER
OFF THE DESK. IT LANDS WITH A CRASH)

MRS BASLOW: Vandals! Stop it! You're mad!

SHE GRABS SUSAN WHO SHAKES HER OFF.
FRANKIE AND LIZ GRAB MRS BASLOW BY
THE ARMS

SUSAN: Mad madams fear not fractured furniture...
(SHE PUSHES OVER DESK. IT ALSO LANDS
WITH A CRASH)

PAT (DISTRAUGHT): Stop it! All of you! Sandra's
gone! Sad Sandra's sure to do herself a mischief!

PANDEMONIUM CHANGES ABRUPTLY TO
AWFUL SILENCE. THE GIRLS LOOK FROM
ONE TO THE OTHER

FRANKIE: The roof! She'll be on the roof!

THEY ALL RUSH OUT, EXIT STAGE LEFT, AS
CURTAIN FALLS

Scene 4

WE HEAR FRENZIED FOOTFALLS, THE
"GIRLS" RE-ENTER STAGE RIGHT IN FRONT
OF CURTAIN, RUN TO CENTRE OF STAGE,

DODGE BACK AND FORTH, LOOKING FOR
SANDRA, BUT ARE STOPPED IN MID-RUN BY
PIERCING SCREAM FROM OFF-STAGE.

FRANKIE (POINTING OUT HIGH OVER
AUDIENCE): There! There she is! There! (SHE
DROPS HER ARM SLOWLY, TRACING
SANDRA'S FALL) There! There! That orange blob
on the car park!

THEY ALL LOOK AWAY IN HORROR

JENNY: We'd better call an ambulance! (TO
AUDIENCE) Oh, who'd have thought it? What could
have made her do it? What makes any person do a
thing like that? (TO THE OTHERS) I think that
Sandra was funny in the head, that's what I think.
(RUSHES OFF STAGE RIGHT)

MRS BASLOW: Sandra! Sandra! You were one of
my pioneers! All eyes were on you and what did you
do? I don't know what the examiners are going to say.
(PAUSE, THEN SCREAM:) Aarrgghh!!! (SHE
COLLAPSES INTO ARMS OF LIZ)

LIZ: I just hope Mrs Baslow's not had a heart attack.
Wake up, Mrs B, wake up! She's just the type. (TO
FRANKIE) Help me undo her collar. God, she's
heavy. Help me. Help me carry her.

FRANKIE (RUSHING TO HELP): We'd better call
two ambulances. (PAUSE, TO AUDIENCE) Well,
she's done it now. That Sandra. She really gave it
everything she'd got, didn't she? Really tried to fly.

SHE AND LIZ DRAG MRS BASLOW OFFSTAGE RIGHT

SUSAN (SHE PICKS SOMETHING OFF HER SLEEVE): Oh. It's my lens. It caught on my sleeve. (PAUSE, THEN SHOUTING AFTER FRANKIE AND LIZ) Wait! Wait for me! (SHE STOPS, TURNS TO AUDIENCE) No reunion then, no getting drunk on sherry. No saying how great it all was. At least (BEAT) now I can use her machine.

SHE ALSO RUNS OFFSTAGE RIGHT, SO ONLY PAT IS LEFT IN FRONT OF THE CURTAIN

PAT (TAKING OUT HER HANKY): Poor Sandra. (SHE WIPES HER EYES AND SLOWLY FOLLOWS THE OTHERS. AS SHE IS ABOUT TO EXIT, SHE TURNS TO THE AUDIENCE): So it wasn't a cry for help after all.

SHE EXITS SLOWLY STAGE RIGHT.
MUSIC: *TOTAL ECLIPSE OF THE HEART* BY BONNIE TYLER

THE END

Other plays by Michael Yates in Nettle Books

The Bronte Boy
(Chosen by the Bronte Society for performance at their annual AGM weekend 2013)
Young Branwell, who once ruled an imaginary childhood world, is now a man, grown mad trying to cope with the real one. As doomed in love as in literature, he slips down the road of drink, drugs and despair. "What the play does brilliantly is the verbal interplay between the principal characters. One feels these are real people, redolent with pithy exchanges and thoughtful thought-provoking dialogue." – Bob Duckett, *Bronte Studies.*
ISBN 978-0-9561513-1-5 Paperback   £6

Short Shorts Vol 1
Three one-act plays including *Life Sentence*, winner of the Stanley Arnold Trophy at the Sheffield One-Act Play Festival.
ISBN 978-0-9561513-3-9 Paperback £6

Short Shorts Vol 2
Three one-act plays including *Luvvies,* described by Manchester's 24:7 Theatre Festival judges as: "A clever, well-written piece. The punchy bitchy dialogue is great fun with an undercurrent of tragedy."
ISBN 978-0-9561513-5-3 Paperback £6

www.ingramcontent.com/pod-product-compliance
Lightning Source LLC
Chambersburg PA
CBHW070806120626
46557CB00002B/736